Hopi overlay bola tie by Fred Kabotie.

# KOKOPELLI

Casanova of the Cliff Dwellers

The hunchbacked flute player

By
John V. Young

**FILTER PRESS**

Palmer Lake, Colorado

1990

# FILTER PRESS
## WILD AND WOOLLY WEST BOOKS

## Post Office Box 95
## Palmer Lake  Colorado   80133
## (719) 481-2420

| | |
|---|---|
| Choda | Thirty Pound Rails, 1956 |
| Clemens | Celebrated Jumping Frog, 1965 |
| Service | Yukon Poems, 1967 |
| Cushing | My Adventures in Zuni, 1967 |
| Matthews | Navajo Weavers and Silversmiths, 1968 |
| Campbell | Wet Plates and Dry Gulches, 1970 |
| Banks | Alferd Packer's Wilderness Cookbook, 1969 |
| Faulk | Simple Methods of Mining Gold, 1969, 1981 |
| Rusho | Powell's Canyon Voyage, 1969 |
| Hinckley | Transcontinental Rails, 1969 |
| Young | The Grand Canyon, 1969 |
| Seig | Tobacco, Peace Pipes and Indians, 1971 |
| Scanland | Life of Pat F. Garrett, 1971 |
| Arpad | Buffalo Bill's Wild West, 1971 |
| Powell | The Hopi Villages, 1972 |
| Hesse | Southwestern Indian Recipe Book, 1973 |
| Schwatka | Among the Apaches, 1974 |
| Bourke & | General Crook in the Indian Country *and* |
| Remington | A Scout with the Buffalo Soldiers, 1974 |
| Powell | An Overland Trip to the Grand Canyon, 1974 |
| Harte | Luck of the Roaring Camp, 1975 |
| Remington | On the Apache Reservations *and* |
| | Among the Cheyennes, 1974 |
| Bryan | Navajo Native Dyes, 1978 |
| Underhill | Pueblo Crafts, 1979 |
| Underhill | Papago & Pima Indians of Arizona, 1979 |
| Bennett | Genuine Navajo Rug; How to Tell, 1979 |
| Duran | Blonde Chicana Bride's Mexican Cookbook, 1981 |
| Kennard | Field Mouse Goes to War, 1977 |
| Keasey | Gadsden's Silent Observers, 1974 |
| Underhill | People of the Crimson Evening, 1982 |
| Choda | West on Wood, Volume 1, 1986 |
| Duran | Mexican Recipe Shortcuts, 1983 |
| Roosevelt | Frontier Types in Cowboy Land, 1988 |
| Young | Kokopelli, 1990 |
| Garrod | Coyote and the Fish, 1993 |
| Williams | Cripple Creek Conflagrations, 1995 |
| Duran | Kid Kokopelli, 1995 |

ISBN  0-86541-026-7

Kokopelli, the traveling salesman, may have used the flute as a notice to villagers that he was coming in peace and was not an enemy sneaking up on them.

Certainly, he has modern counterparts. In Belize, Central America, a group of peddlers take back trails into the remote towns and villages, riding bicycles! They are known as Cobaneros, since many start from the Guatemalan city of Coban. Their predecessors carried shell and tropical goods to the northern pueblos, trading for turquoise. The Cobaneros bring small consumer goods, some textiles, and trade for money. Today they are considered smugglers. Earlier they were not as there were no national boundaries.

Kokopelli is becoming more popular as "yard art". Wrought iron and steel cutouts adorn lawns in Santa Fe and Albuquerque. In Tucson, the security grille of Bahti's Indian Arts has wrought iron replicas of Kokopelli among images of many pictographs and petroglyphs.

As "Water Sprinkler" Kokopelli was a benign minor god, bringing abundant rain and food to the People.

Kokopelli in Chaco Canyon. after Waters

A bicycle trail is being built between the Grand Canyon and Aspen, Colorado. The first section of Kokopelli's Trail® now reaches from Grand Junction, Colorado to Moab, Utah.

Built as a joint effort of the Colorado Plateau Mountain Bike Trail Association, the Bureau of Land Management, and the U.S. Forest Service, it was blessed by a delegation of Hopi Indians from Arizona.

The trail markers show Kokopelli, with a bicycle and mountains in the background.

Gilbert L. Campbell
Publisher

Hunchback flute player in cave on Pajarito Plateau, west of Santa Fe. "Spear Point" may be later addition by vandals.

# ILLUSTRATIONS

Photographs are by the author. Heather Hamilton has prepared drawings and sketches from other sources cited.

Paul and Diana LeMarbe have provided illustrations from their Southwest Sun screen printed fabrics.

Other illustrations are from early travel and scientific books and publications of the late 19th century.

Gila Bend Kokopelli. Compare with Chaco and Oraibi. after Waters

Faded by time and weathering, flute player among petroglyphs in Rio Grande Canyon between Los Alamos and Santa Fe. Note recent addition of plumed serpent.

# Preface

Everywhere that primitive man roamed the American Southwest, as well as in many other places in the world, he left an enduring record of his passing fancies and urgencies in the form of pictures on rocks.

Those painted on rock surfaces are called pictographs. Those incised in the rock surface by pecking or scratching with a stone tool are called petroglyphs. To us, many of the designs are undecipherable, but many others seem to be more or less obvious representations of deer, antelope, bighorn sheep, bears, wolves, coyotes, buffalo, turkeys, cranes, serpents, frogs, lizards and insects.

Hands and feet often appear, sometimes with six digits. Figures of men are depicted fighting, hunting, or apparently doing nothing at all. Other designs almost certainly represent the sun, moon, stars, lightning, clouds, rain and corn — always corn, that sacred and indispensable New World grain originally known as maize. Some signs tell of water springs, trails or the abode of spirits. Others could be rebus writing: the representation of words by pictures of objects whose names sound (in the aboriginal language) like the intended words, as in our parlor game of charades.

The Flute player in Oraibi is much like those at Gila Bend and Chaco.
after Waters.

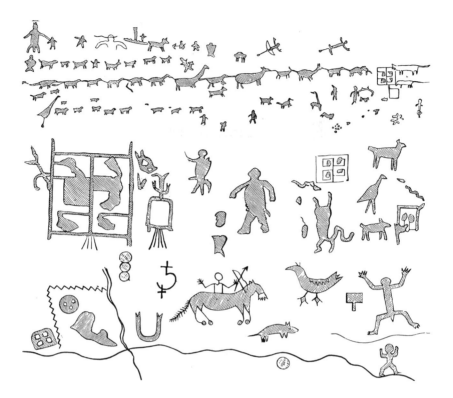

Old wood engraving of "Rock Inscriptions", El Morro. Thayer, 1893

El Morro, now Inscription Rock National Monument, near Gallup.  Thayer, 1893.

Why did the ancient people go to all that trouble? As a guess, some of the symbols were intended to invoke good or to repel evil, to assure a crop or to assist in childbirth. But probably nobody will ever know for certain what all of the Southwest's millions of pictographs and petroglyphs were supposed to mean or to do, since they never attained the status of a written language.

Many of the figures might well have been nothing more than the product of idle doodling by people with time on their hands and a smooth surface to scribble on. People still do it, but now usually it is called graffiti.

Newspaper Rock State Park, Utah displays hundreds of petroglyphs under cliff overhang.

# Casanova of the Ancient Ones

## The hunchbacked flute player

Of the multitude of miscellaneous drawings, paintings and scratchings on the rocks and in the caves of the pre-Columbian people of the Southwest, only one anthropomorphic subject can claim both an identity and a proper name as well as gender. Without question, that figure is decidedly male.

Kokopelli's frequent and widespread appearance on pottery and in pictography suggest that he was a well-travelled and universally recognized deity of considerable potency.

A personality, an individual, the personification of a legend, a beneficent god to some and a confounded nuisance to others, such is Kokopelli, the famous hunchbacked flute player, the Kilroy of the Hohokam, thousands of years old but figuratively speaking very much in the present.

Kokopelli, followed by his wife Kokopelli-mana, embellishes a Hohokam bowl from Snaketown, Arizona. after Gladwin

1

Present-day pottery-makers, weavers and painters often use the figure as a decoration, perhaps in many instances with no knowledge of the history or the significance of the representation. Fortunately, Kokopelli has never been a sinister character, never voodooistic, but frequently comic.

Kokopelli appears from the San Juan Basin and Monument Valley to Casas Grandes in Mexico, among the Navajos, the Hopis, the Rio Grande pueblos and others westward to desert California. Not surprisingly, his phallic figure is among the thousands at Arizona's Painted Rocks State Park on the Gila River west of Gila Bend. Early Spanish explorers made note of the rock carvings and called them "piedras pintadas" or painted rocks, although the pictographs actually are incised or scratched rather than painted. Early explorers, trappers and hunters were not noted for their verbal precision.

Kokopelli on a screenprinted Tee shirt by Southwest Sun of Columbus, New Mexico.

"Paintings" on the rocks of Piedras Pintadas in Arizona.  Browne 1869.

Kokopelli's likeness varies almost as much as the legends about him, but by and large he is unmistakable, grotesquely hunchbacked, usually phallic in the extreme, and nearly always playing some sort of flute or flageolet.

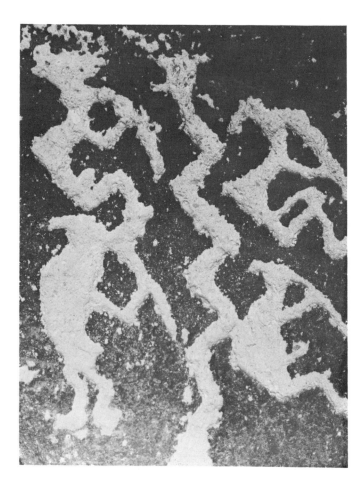

Group of four crude flute players and plumed serpent in cave high in canyon wall, Los Alamos county, N.M. Smoke on white pumice cave wall contrasts with scratched image.

While some authorities say the flute is a blow-gun, advocates of the musical instrument theory are in the majority. Man has been tootling through a nose pipe since the late Stone Age, virtually all over the world. Usually a man's instrument forbidden to women, a tube of reed, bone or wood similar to the mouth flute was played by blowing nostril breath through one end.

Natives of Tahiti used to close one nostril with the thumb while waggling the other fingers along note holes in the tube. Some clans preferred the left nostril, others the right. Some anthropologists surmise that nose music arose from the belief of primitive man that the soul or life-spirit entered and left the body through the nose. The exclamation "God bless you!" — uttered when a person sneezes — may be rooted in the same belief, that nostril breath possesses magical powers.

The Kokopelli figure has been found in ruins of pithouse people dating as early as 200 A.D., and as late as the 16th century where it appears in association with drawings of men on horseback, men armored and men in cowls.

Southwest sun fabric design.

Silver earring enlarged 50%

HLH

5

Arrival of the Spanish conquistadores and missionaries did more than establish an historical date as a base. Through the Inquisition, slavery, starvation and disease, the natives were all but obliterated. Life in the Southwest was never again the same for Kokopelli and his people.

Before the arrival of the Spaniards, however, pinning down historical dates becomes difficult to the point of impossibility. Something can be learned from the chemistry of the petroglyphs etched on the smooth faces of basaltic cliffs and caves. The drawings are pecked or scratched through the dark brown patina known as desert varnish, the product of centuries of slow oxidation of the minerals in the rock. The artwork exposes lighter-colored rock beneath the patina. Then, over the centuries, the lighter-colored rock will darken again, and in time becomes virtually invisible.

Small figure of Kokopelli at San Cristobal ruin.

6

Casual scratchings by vandals are readily apparent because of their color and may be erased by park staff, as have those at Utah's Newspaper Rock State Park. Displaying thousands of figures, the rocks obviously served as a kind of bulletin board for people with no written alphabet.

Detail of figures on Newspaper Rock

Seated turtle like figure is possible variation of Kokopelli often found
on Hopi pottery. This group is near San Cristobal ruins southeast of
Santa Fe in the Galisteo Basin.

Two of the figures appear to be much older than the others, since they have become much darker than their neighbors. Also, the carvings must have been made when the flood plain at the base of the rock was much higher than it is now. Erosion of the terrain over the centuries has left the top of the rock high and dry, and quite inaccessible without tall ladders.

Another notable feature 'of the Newspaper Rock carvings is the presence of large, six-toed feet, suggesting that there may have been a clan or family of six-toed people who were regarded as gods or in any case worthy of being reported on the rock. The scientific term for six-toes is polydactylic, which does not help much since it simply means many digits.

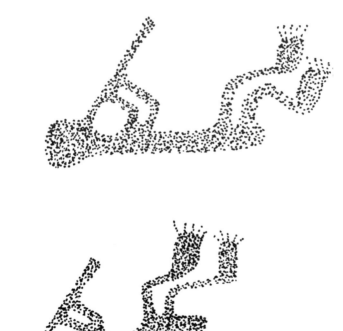

A pair of recumbent figures in Tse-Begay, Monument Valley.
After Campbell photo

Now back to Kokopelli, whose outstanding feature was **not** his feet.

The reason Kokopelli has a name is fairly simple. The Hopi people of central Arizona, aptly called "archeology on the hoof," make a variety of kachina dolls to sell to tourists. Among the dolls is one they call Kokopelli, and his "wife" is called Kokopelli-mana. Koko is hunchbacked and plays a flute. Formerly he was vividly phallic, but the missionaries persuaded the Indians to omit this feature in the interests of what they (the missionaries) called decency. The Hopis did not consider sex to be indecent — merely absurd.

Petroglyph of Kokopelli & Shield-Sun?  Volcano Cliffs near Albuquerque.                    After Campbell photo

Another recumbent Kokopelli, Monument Valley After Campbell

Like most genuine Kachinas, Kokopelli used to have a human counterpart in a Kachina dancer, the personification of a giant who lived in the mountains. What Kokopelli used to do with explicit gestures to the missionary ladies and female tourists before they learned what the gestures meant, and why the Indians were convulsed with mirth, would be worth elucidating.

Kokopelli's exaggerated phallic appearance could have been due to priapism* or to tuberculosis, or more likely to the common superstition that holds all hunchbacks to be fertility symbols. Many primitive peoples welcomed Kokopelli around corn-planting time. Barren wives sought his company; unmarried maidens fled from him in terror.

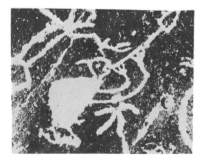

Los Alamos County, New Mexico

* Priapus, in both Greek and Roman ancient religious lore, was a fertility god of gardens and herds, the son of Aphrodite and Dionysus. He was depicted as a grotesque little man with an enormous phallus, obviously important in fertility rites.

11

Two small dancing figures are probably versions of Kokopelli without the flute. These are among many petroglyphs in the San Cristobal ruins.

Oraibi women and maiden preparing food. Powell, 1875

13

The name Kokopelli may derive from Zuni and Hopi names for a god (Koko), and a desert robber fly they call pelli. That predatory insect has a hump on his back and some deplorable habits such as stealing the larvae of other flies. The flute could be the insect's prominent proboscis. Some of the drawings on pottery of the Hohokam and Mimbres people of prehistoric southern Arizona look more like the insect than the man.

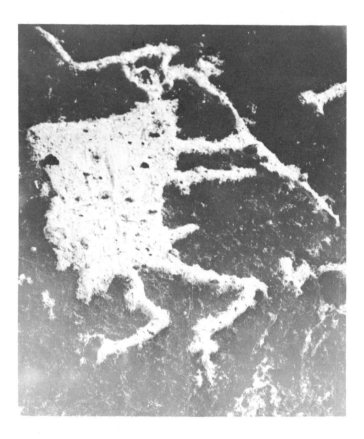

Angular version of Kokopelli in cave on the Pajarito Plateau. Note how the long horn suggests an insect.

However, it is among the present-day Pueblo people of New Mexico and Arizona that the bulk of the Kokopelli legends were still current until fairly recent times. At San Ildefonso, he was known as a wandering minstrel with a sack of songs on his back. In the Aladdin tradition, he traded new songs for old, and was greeted as a harbinger of fertility and a god of the harvest.

The old South Kiva at San Ildefonso.  After Campbell photo

At Hano, on the Hopi First Mesa, occupied by Pueblo refugees from central New Mexico, Kokopelli and his wife are painted black. He is said to be a character they call **Neopkwai'i** which means "big black man". This could be none other than Esteban, the giant Moor who guided Fray Marcos de Niza and his party on their ill-fated exploration of southern Arizona in 1539. Esteban was more interested in the comely Zuni women than he was in the fabled Seven Cities of Cibola the party was seeking. When he made passes at the girls, the men decided he was no god after all and shot him full of arrows. Then they buried him under a pile of rocks.

Watching from a safe distance, Marcos de Niza and the rest of the party hastily erected a cross and then took off for Mexico City where they had some hairy tales to tell.

15

Doorway and ruined wall at Hano, Hopi First Mesa. Mindeleef, 1891.

A terrace view of Zuni Pueblo.  Cushing 1883.

At Oraibi, another Hopi village, Kokopelli is said to have a sack of deerskin shirts and moccasins to barter for brides, a modified version of the Esteban legend. Elsewhere among the Hopis he is said to spend his time sewing on shirts and seducing the daughters of the household while his wife, Kokopelli-mana, runs after the men.

Kokopelli figures prominently in the obscure Blue Feather legend of the Navajos. This ancient tale says that a wandering Zuni named Blue Feather who was very skillful with throwing sticks (used like dice), bankrupted the great city of Pueblo Bonito in Chaco Canyon (now a national historic park). This action led to the city's downfall in the 13th century, the story goes. Not satisfied with winning all the tribal treasure and lands, Blue Feather took over the running of the city. His delusions of grandeur led him to woo and win one of the city's sacred vestal virgins. This act of sacrilege brought down the terrible wrath of the gods in the form of drought and disease. The surviving people all ran away and the city collapsed, leaving Blue Feather buried in the ruins.

As man-servant to Blue Feather and bodyguard for the heroine of the piece, the hunchback Kokopelli either died in the ruins with his master, or ran off with the girl according to which version you prefer.

Quartet or Jam Session?     Southwest Sun

Ruins in Canyon de Chelly     Bickford 1890

The Navajo tribe owns and guards one of the finest arrays of Kokopelli figures ever discovered. A long frieze of hunchbacked flute players adorns a large boulder sheltering a small ruin in a remote part of Monument Valley. The ruin was named Flute Player House by the archaeologists who excavated it in 1920.

The real origin of these symbols, like other relics of the arcane Indian world, may be futile to seek in 20th century Anglo-Saxon terms and modes of thought. Perhaps there really was a hunchbacked minstrel with an eye for the girls somewhere in the dim past, whose memory has come down through the ages like that of the Wandering Jew. Or perhaps the same legend sprang up simultaneously among disparate people with no contact, although this seems unlikely. In any case, the notion of a footloose and hunchbacked flute player with the gift of fertility must have satisfied some deep yearning of the ancient people or they would not have nurtured the legend all the way down to the present day.

House of chief Talti, Oraibi.   Powell 1875

White House Ruin in Canyon de Chelly.  Bickford, 1890

The wrought iron security grille, Bahti's Indian Arts, Tucson.

# BIBLIOGRAPHY

Anasazi, Ancient People of the Rock.
  Photos by David Muench, text by Donald G. Pike, Palo
  Alto, American West Publishing Co., 1974.

Bickford, F. T.
  Prehistoric Cave Dwellings. *Century v.40 (ns 18):896-911,
  1890.*

Browne, J. Ross
  Adventures in the Apache Country. *Harper's Monthly,
  30, Oct 1864-Mar 1865.* Also reprinted U. of Arizona I
  Press, 1974.

Cushing, Frank H.
  My Adventures in Zuni. *Century, vols 25,26, 1883,1884.*
  also Filter Press, 1967.

Cushing, Frank H.
  Zuni Fetishes. Las Vegas, KC Publications, 1966.

HLH

At Volcano Cliffs, Albuquerque, Kokopelli with horns resembles
Navajo Hunchback God.                    After Campbell photo

High walls and ladder, Hano, First Mesa Hopi village.  Powell 1875.

24

Gladwin, Harold S.
A History of the Ancient Southwest. Portland, Bond Wheelwright, 1957.

Grant, Campbell
Rock Art of the American Indian. NY Crowell, 1967.

Hawley, F.
Kokopelli of the Southwestern Indian Pantheon. *American Anthropologist. 39:644-46, 1937.*

Mead, George
Rock Art north of the Mexican border. Greeley, Museum of Anthropology. *Occasional publications in Anthropology Archeological Series No. 5, 1968.*

Mindeleff, Victor A.
A study of Pueblo Architecture, Tusayan and Cibola a Washington, Bureau of Ethnology 8th Ann. Rept.,1891

Packard, Gar
Suns and Serpents. Santa Fe, Packard Pubs., 1974.

In the Galisteo Basin Kokopelli seems to be wearing a helmet and blowing a horn rather than a flute. A shield or sun symbol is in front of him.                                    After Muench

Mummy Cave and ruin, Canyon del Muerto.   Bickford, 1890

Parsons, E. C.
The Humpbacked flute player of the Southwest. *American Anthropologist 40:337-388, 1938.*

Powell, John Wesley
Ancient Province of Tusayan.*Scribners Monthly :193-213, Dec, 1875.*

Renaud, E.B.
. Kokopelli, a study in Pueblo mythology. *Southwestern Lore 14:25-40, 1948.*

Schaafsma, Polly,
Early Navaho Rock Painting and Carvings, Santa Fe Museum of Navaho Ceremonial Art, 1966.

Schaafsma, Polly
Southwest Indian Pictographs and Petroglyphs. Santa Fe Museum of New Mexico Press, 1965.

HLH

A potbellied Kokopelli toots another horn, St Johns, Arizona.
After Waters

Tanner, Clara Lee
Prehistoric Southwestern Craft Arts, Tucson, University of Arizona Press, 1976.

Thayer, William M.
Marvels of the New West. Norwich, Conn., Bill Publishing Co., 1892.

Titiev, M.
Story of Kokopelli. *American Anthropologist 41:91-98,1939.*

Waters, Frank, and Oswald White Bear Fredericks.
Book of the Hopi. NY Viking, 1963.

Wellmann, Klaus F.
Kokopelli of Indian Paleology. *Journal of the American Medical Association 212:1678-1682, June 8, 1970*

Young, John V.
Peregrinations of Kokopelli. *Westways (L.A.) 57 no 9:39-41, Sept. 1965.*

HLH

Almost identical recumbent figures in Sonora, Mexico (above) and in Canyon de Chelly, Arizona, suggest a Kokopelli resting at home. The Mexican figure, found in a cave, is almost ten feet long. After Waters.

This horned Kokopelli from Cieneguita, New Mexico may be the Navajo Hunchback god, who carries a spear or wand, and a pack of seeds on his back. He is also called Water Sprinkler.

after Renaud